To lovely Lottie (and Cloth and Rabbity).
-A.S.

For Maya, who will soon be big enough, too.
-L.M

Text copyright © 2007 Amber Stewart • Illustrations copyright © 2007 Layn Marlow

First published in the U.S.A. by Orchard Books. All rights reserved.

Published by Orchard Books, an imprint of Scholastic Inc, *Publishers since 1920*.

ORCHARD BOOKS and design are registered trademarks of Watts Publishing Group, Ltd., used under license.

SCHOLASTIC and associated logos are trademarks and/or registered trademarks of Scholastic Inc. • No part of this publication may be reproduced, stored in a retrieval system, or transmitted in any form or by any means, electronic, mechanical, photocopying, recording, or otherwise, without written permission of the publisher. • For information regarding permission, write to Orchard Books, Scholastic Inc., Attention: Permissions Department, 557 Broadway, New York, NY 10012. • Library of Congress Cataloging-in-Publication Data • Stewart, Amber I'm Big Enough / by Amber Stewart; illustrated by Layn Marlow.—1st Scholastic ed. p. cm. Summary: Although she is getting bigger every day, Bean the rabbit refuses to give up her blanket. [1. Blankets—Fiction. 2. Growth—Fiction. 3. Rabbits—Fiction.] I. Marlow, Layn, ill. II. Title. III. Title: I am big enough. PZ7.S84868Im 2007 [E]—dc22 2006017193 ISBN-13: 978-0-439-90666-1 • ISBN-10: 0-439-90666-0 (alk. paper) • 10 9 8 7 6 5 4 3 2 1   07 08 09 10 11 / • Printed in China Reinforced Binding for Library Use • First Scholastic edition, March 2007 • Book design by Alison Klapthor

Amber Stewart & Layn Marlow

I'm Big Enough

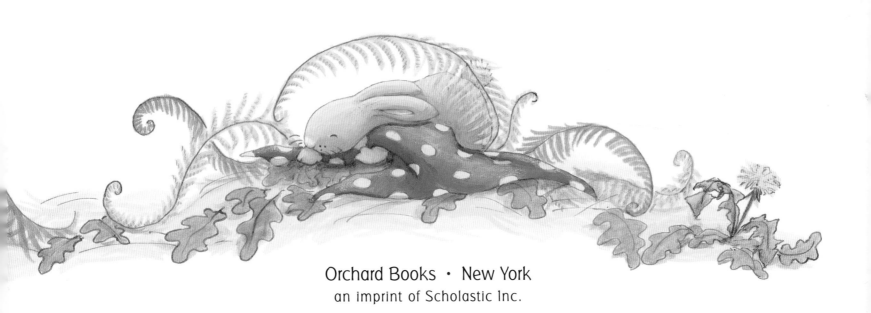

Orchard Books · New York
an imprint of Scholastic Inc.

Bean was big enough.

She was big enough to hop all the
way around Stickleback Pond
without stopping.

She was big enough to go dandelion
picking and to choose the juiciest ones
for Mommy to cook.

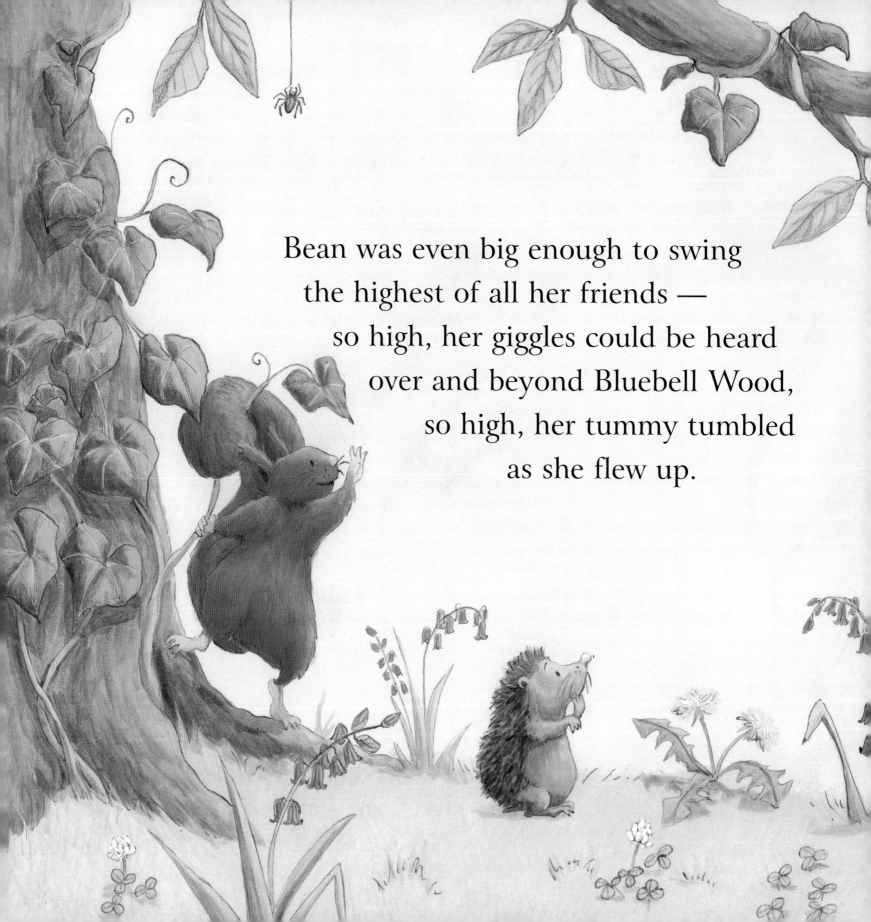

Bean was even big enough to swing
the highest of all her friends —
so high, her giggles could be heard
over and beyond Bluebell Wood,
so high, her tummy tumbled
as she flew up.

She was big enough to do
all these things,

but was Bean big enough to stop
taking her blanket just about
everywhere she went?

"No," said Bean. "I love my Blankie."

"Maybe you could try doing things without your blanket?" said Mommy and Daddy gently.

"Yes — blankets are for babies," said Bean's big brother.

"No they're not," said Bean.

So Bean made a plan just in case her family decided to take her blanket away. She called it the "Keep Blankie Forever Plan."

Early in the morning,
Bean set out to hide her
blanket in a special secret place.

It wasn't on the edge of
Stickleback Pond because
the frogs might find it.

It wasn't between the branches
of Thunderstruck Tree because
the birds might take it.

It wasn't buried in the
soft earth because the
mice might want it.

Bean was just wondering if she would ever find the right spot, when she saw a hollow log hidden by overgrown bushes.

Bean hid her blanket deep in the hollow log —
and hurried home. She was happy all
day knowing that the blanket was safe.

But when bedtime drew near, Bean
wanted her blanket. She had never had
a bedtime without cuddling her blanket,
and she didn't want one now.

So Bean set out to her secret hiding
place to bring her blanket back home.

The woods looked different in the early evening light.
All the hollow logs seemed the same, and now
Bean wasn't sure which one

was her hiding place.

Was her blanket in that
hollow log . . .

or that one . . .

or that one?

"Oh no!" cried Bean.
"My plan didn't work.
I've lost Blankie!"

Poor Bean had no choice but to return home.
Blanket-less, and close to tears, she saw Mommy.

"Bean, where did you go?" Mommy asked.
"To look for Blankie," sniffed Bean,
"but I couldn't find it."

Bean's family was very kind about the
lost blanket disaster.

Daddy read her two extra bedtime stories, and
Mommy made her hot milk to help her sleep.
And Bean's brother lent her his
second favorite teddy bear.

Bean didn't like her
first bedtime without
her blanket. She didn't
much like her second,
or third, either.

But soon, looking for
her blanket turned into
looking for ladybugs
and four-leaf clovers . . .

and making the very
best hideouts . . .

and going hollow-log
sledding . . .

until Bean had forgotten all about her blanket.

One windy spring day, a long time later,
Bean and her friends were chasing dandelion
seeds in a sunny part of the woods, when
she saw the strangest thing. . .

Bean looked at the tiny baby fox and knew
now that her mommy was right —
she really was much too big
for her blanket.